BLOOD ON SNOW

A DETECTIVE KAY HUNTER SHORT STORY

RACHEL AMPHLETT

Copyright © 2020 by Rachel Amphlett

All rights reserved.

No part of this book may be reproduced in any form or by any electronic or mechanical means, including information storage and retrieval systems, without written permission from the author, except for the use of brief quotations in a book review.

This is a work of fiction. While the locations in this book are a mixture of real and imagined, the characters are totally fictitious. Any resemblance to actual people living or dead is entirely coincidental.

FOREWORD

The Detective Kay Hunter series is enthralling murder mystery readers with its fast-paced and entertaining storylines that provide a modern twist to the police procedural genre.

The full-length novels are available through all major retailers and local libraries in eBook, print and audiobook.

These short stories follow Kay Hunter's early years as a probationary detective constable and can be read in any order. The stories form part of the new *Case Files* series of pocket-sized murder mysteries from USA Today bestselling author Rachel Amphlett.

For more information about this series and more, visit www.rachelamphlett.com.

BLOOD ON SNOW

ONE

The car slewed to a begrudging standstill, the tyres sinking into fresh snow two inches thick and unspoilt.

Beyond the windscreen stood a modest three-bedroom suburban home with a white topping of flakes covering the roof tiles, icicle-shaped Christmas fairy lights dangling from the windowsills battling for space with the real thing.

The middle house was identical to four others in the small crescent-shaped street – except for the uniformed police officers and white-suited crime scene investigators crowding the driveway and postage stamp-sized front garden.

To the left of the vehicle, separating the crescent from the busy main road, was a grass-covered area housing a council rubbish bin and a bus shelter.

The grass had been churned up into a mixture of snow and mud – no doubt a snowball fight had been underway earlier that morning. A group of children held aloft mobile phones while they walked towards the secondary school farther along the road, their expressions bored rather than curious.

Probationary Detective Constable Kay Hunter paused with her hand on the car door handle and turned to her colleague, wool from her navy scarf sticking to her chapped lips before she brushed it out of the way.

'What do we know so far?'

Police Constable Simon Higgins tucked his radio into his stab vest and reached for his hat. 'The first responders got here half an hour ago. A woman, Liz Carter, was found dead in her back garden. The husband phoned 999 at ten past eight. They've got two teenagers – a boy of thirteen, and a fifteen-year-old daughter.'

'Bloody hell.' Kay heaved the door open, a blast of ice cold air filling the vehicle. 'Okay, let's go and find Sharp.'

Her foot slipped on the icy surface of the road as she got out, and she threw her hands out to the sides to regain her balance before falling into step beside Higgins.

She flashed her warrant card to the young PC guarding the taped-off concrete driveway, then signed the crime scene log he held out.

'Kay, we're through here.'

Detective Sergeant Devon Sharp waited at the front door, beckoning to her.

Ex-military police, ramrod straight with the first signs of grey at his temples, he stood to one side as she entered a bright hallway decorated with tinsel pinned in zigzag patterns across the ceiling.

Low voices mumbled through a door to her left, while two abandoned backpacks lay next to the bottom tread of the staircase on her right.

'DC Christie's speaking to the husband and kids,' Sharp murmured. 'Come through to the kitchen and I'll show you what we've got so far.'

Kay kept her hands shoved in her pockets and followed him, her gaze roaming the family photographs hanging on the wall as she passed.

Liz Carter was a stylish brunette in her forties and in all the pictures had her arms draped around two kids who shared her toothy smile. Beside them, Andrew Carter towered above his wife, his close-cropped hair doing little to disguise a receding hairline.

Turning away at the sound of a polite cough, Kay edged sideways to let a CSI technician pass then blinked as she recognised the lanky form of Hugh Hughes.

'I didn't know you were at work this week,' she said.

'This morning,' Hugh replied, peering over his glasses at her as he pulled away his mask. 'Hell of a way to start the day.'

'Kay?'

She hurried to catch up with Sharp, entering a light and airy kitchen that appeared to have had a recent renovation.

A centre worktop ran the length of the room and led to patio doors, both of which were open.

She shivered, and followed her DS as he strode out into the garden and paused beside three stone steps bordered with snow-topped shrubs.

A second cordon of crime tape separated them from a team of four CSIs who crouched a few yards from where Kay stood, their backs to her as they trod a demarcated path between the house and the woman's body.

'You missed Lucas,' said Sharp. 'He got

another call out near Sheppey, but he reckons she died from a single blow to the head.'

Kay winced. 'Did she die straight away?'

'You know what these Home Office pathologists are like. He won't confirm it until after he's conducted the post mortem tomorrow morning but he thinks it was instant, yes.'

He moved to one side, and Kay swallowed.

Liz Carter lay on her back, her blank eyes staring up at the grey sky, a strand of hair across her forehead matted with viscous blood that had splattered the front of her shirt. Her arms were outstretched like a snow angel as if she tried to break her fall, her mouth open in shock.

Kay wanted to wrap the woman in a soft blanket to shield her from the biting wind, noting she only wore slip-on patent shoes that matched her tailored suit trousers.

'Have they found a weapon?'

'Not yet.' Sharp peered over her shoulder. 'Here's Richard.'

Kay turned as DC Christie walked out of the kitchen and headed towards them, his face grim. 'The husband, Andrew, says he was in the shower when it happened. The two kids – Michael and Stephanie – were in the living room eating breakfast and watching television. Andrew noticed the back doors were open when he came downstairs, and that's when he found his wife.'

'Did he have any idea what she was doing out here?' said Sharp.

'They adopted a cat last week. Apparently it kept getting out and she was afraid it'd go missing if it escaped.' Christie snapped shut his notebook. 'He thinks she went out after it to get it to come back inside before they went to work.'

Turning back to face the garden, Sharp let out a sigh. 'All right, you two. No sign of a weapon, and this garden isn't accessible via a gate. The only way in and out of here is through the house.'

'The kids say they had the living room door open while they were having breakfast,' said Christie. 'No-one came in through the front door – and Andrew confirms it was locked anyway. It always is until they leave to go to work and drop the kids off to school.'

'Jesse!'

A girl's voice shouted from inside the house a split second before a tabby-coloured blur shot past Kay's legs and onto the snow-covered lawn.

'Christ, there goes the crime scene,' said

Sharp as the four CSIs rose to their feet and tried to usher the cat away from the taped-off area.

Kay spun around at the sound of footsteps and closed the patio doors as a teenaged girl slid to a halt on the tiled floor.

Shaking her head, holding out her arms to try to block the view of the garden, Kay waited until Andrew Carter guided his daughter away, and bit back a sigh of relief.

'Did she see?' Sharp's voice held a note of panic.

'I don't think so.' Kay straightened her coat and walked over to where the DS and Christie stood on the steps, their faces concerned. 'I think I got there in time.'

'Thank God for that.'

Kay sidled closer, peering past his shoulder to where one of the CSIs was wrestling with the cat in his arms, a fresh trail of paw prints covering the snowy ground.

She frowned. 'Sarge? No-one else has walked on that snow except the husband and the wife, right? Besides the cat, I mean.'

Sharp moved until he was standing next to her. 'That's right – the CSIs stuck to the demarcated path.'

'Then where are the killer's footprints?'

TWO

'Someone get that bloody camera crew away from here,' Sharp barked, his voice carrying over the uniformed officers milling about the front garden. 'And tell the Family Liaison Officer to close the living room curtains.'

He turned to Kay and Christie. 'Right, you two – split up and start talking to the neighbours. Kay, you take Higgins with you and speak to the owners of the house at the back of the Carters' home – the gardens border each other, so our killer may have escaped that way. Christie, you're with me – we'll start with next door, number four. Apparently the bloke at number two on the other side works night shifts and isn't home yet.'

'Okay, Sarge.' Kay wandered across the driveway to where Higgins hovered at the outer perimeter, and jerked her thumb over her shoulder. 'Simon, you're with me. Sharp wants us to interview the neighbours in the house behind this one.'

'Do you want to take the car?'

She took one look at the traffic streaming along the street beyond the crescent and the emergency vehicles clogging the kerb, and shook her head. 'It'll be quicker if we walk.'

Reaching the entrance to the crescent, she paused and extracted her notebook from her bag, then drew the cluster of five houses arching left to right, added the house numbers and put a pencil mark next to the Carters' house.

That done, she glanced up to see Higgins watching.

'Just getting my bearings,' she said.

'Does Sharp think the killer got away through one of the other gardens?'

'Maybe. Let's go.'

She kept up with the quick pace he set, taking care to avoid icy patches that were beginning to appear on the pavement as the snow melted under passing foot traffic.

They turned into a dead-end street that ran behind the crescent, the properties spaced farther apart than the neighbouring streets and with large gardens and driveways that swept out of sight behind brick walls or privet hedges. Here, the snow was thicker on the pavements, the tyre tracks in the road favouring the left-hand side as residents had negotiated the icy conditions to begin their morning commute.

'This is the one.' Kay paused outside a mock-Tudor home, a gravel path leading to the front door.

Edging past a modern-looking camper van parked outside the garage, she rang the bell beside a glass-panelled door and took a step back, eyeing the six-foot-high fencing that stretched from each side of the house, shielding the back garden from view.

A fuzzy shape emerged from behind the glass before the door swung open and a man in his sixties peered out at them, his expression confused.

'We're not interested in buying anything, whatever it is you're selling.'

Kay held up her warrant card. 'Mr—'

'Hugh Starling.'

'Detective Constable Kay Hunter, and this is my colleague PC Simon Higgins. We were wondering if we could have a word, please?'

'What's this about?'

'I'm sorry, sir, but we're investigating the suspicious death of one of your neighbours,' said Kay, keeping her tone steady. 'Liz Carter.'

'Liz? Oh… oh my goodness.' Starling moved to one side. 'Come in, please. Don't worry about taking off your shoes. We can go through to the kitchen.'

Kay wiped her feet on the coir mat then stepped inside, her shoes clattering on the laminate flooring as she shuffled to one side to let Higgins in after her.

An immediate warmth caressed her cheeks, and she unbuttoned her coat and loosened her scarf while Starling shut the door and gestured towards the back of the house.

'Beverley just put the kettle on. Would you like a hot drink?'

'No, that's kind but we won't keep you long,' said Kay, and nodded to a woman hovering beside a worktop, her grey hair bunched up on top of her head and secured with various pins.

'Love, Detective Hunter and her colleague say that Liz Carter was killed this morning,' said Hugh, moving closer to his wife and then placing a hand around her waist.

'Liz? Murdered?' Beverley's eyes widened as she raised a shaking hand to her mouth.

'We can't say for sure at the moment,' said

Kay. 'We are treating her death as suspicious, though. How long have you known them?'

'About five years,' said Hugh. 'We moved here when I sold my plumbing business and took early retirement. The trees out the back weren't so big then, so we'd often stop to chat over the back fence.'

Running her eyes over a large pinewood table set to one side of the kitchen, Kay noted its surface was covered with plastic parts and paint pots.

A strong acetone smell filled the air as Beverley Starling flipped on an extractor hood above the stove top and rolled her eyes.

'I keep telling him the fumes are dangerous, but he won't listen,' she said.

Kay wandered over to the table, her interest piqued by the model aircraft taking shape. 'What are you making?'

'A Mark IX Spitfire,' said Hugh, his voice full of pride. 'I should have it finished by Christmas.'

'By which time, he's hoping the family will buy him some more kits to make in the New Year,' said his wife, her tone indulgent. 'Maybe another radio-controlled boat or something.'

'What about you, Mrs Starling – any hobbies?' said Higgins.

'Oh, just craft things. Needlework, that sort of thing. I knit blankets for the local rescue shelter.'

'Bev and I tend to call these our winter projects,' said Hugh. 'In the summer, we travel around quite a bit.'

'The camper van outside?' said Kay.

'We've been to eight different countries in it so far,' he beamed.

'Could I take a look at your back garden please?'

'Of course.' Beverley ushered her through a utility room that carried a heady aroma of cat litter, laundry powder and damp socks.

Kay passed a pair of work boots drying out on an old newspaper, water soaking into the print, and then followed the woman out into the garden.

A path ran behind the house, the crunch of gravel audible under a soft layer of snow as Kay wandered away from Beverley, leaving the woman huddled in her thick cardigan at the back door.

Beyond a landscaped terrace cluttered with an ice-filled bird bath and various seed dispensers hanging from metal stakes was a wide snow-covered lawn stretching the length of two of the neighbouring properties before it gave way to a border of thick hawthorn hedgerows and leylandii trees. A wooden shed had been built in the far left corner of the garden, a variety of composting bins and a water butt nestled beside it.

To the right and between the branches, Kay could see the red tiled rooftop of the Carters' house.

Footprints tracked back and forth in the snow, but none went as far as the hedgerow.

'Whose are those?' she said, turning back to the house.

Higgins had emerged with Hugh Starling beside him, his gaze travelling over to where Kay pointed.

'Mine,' said Hugh. 'I was outside earlier shovelling snow off the path and put some more food out for the birds.'

'What time was that?' said Higgins, his notebook already open.

'About eight o'clock, I think.' Hugh's brow furrowed. 'Yes, eight. The news was about to start on the radio – I could hear the pips on the hour as I went out the back door with the food scraps from last night to put them in the compost bin over by the shed.'

'I-I can't believe this is happening. They're such a nice family,' said Beverley, dabbing at her eyes with her sleeve. 'The kids, too –

always said hello if we bumped into them in the shop down the road or out and about.'

Hugh's mouth twisted. 'She's right. Much better than the idiot on the other side of the fence.'

'Oh?' Kay pulled out her notebook and flipped to the sketch of the crescent. 'That would be number…'

'Two,' said Hugh, 'and a pain in the backside – especially in the summer with his loud parties.'

'You can smell the marijuana from here,' Beverley sniffed. 'I think Andrew and Liz told him to keep the music down a few times, too.'

'Did you see anyone else while you were out here earlier, Mr Starling?' said Higgins.

'No, I didn't.'

'Do you think the murderer escaped through our garden?' Beverley's eyes widened as she turned to her husband and reached out her hand. 'Oh my God. You might've been in danger.'

'It's too early to say, Mrs Starling,' said Kay. 'I'll take some photos though, if that's all right with you?'

Hugh waved her onwards, leading his wife back into the house as Higgins joined her.

'What do you think, Kay?' he said. 'First impressions?'

She bit her lip, lowered the phone and then took a deep breath.

'I don't think our killer escaped through here. There's only the one set of footprints and no sign of anyone else being here. If someone climbed over the fence and through that hedgerow or over the shed roof, I'd expect to see prints, perhaps an imprint of someone landing after a fall—'

'Right, and Starling told me the side gate has a padlock on it. I checked – no-one went through there this morning, and they didn't go over the top of the fence into the front garden from here, either – there's still snow lining the top of it. Not a smudge in sight.'

Kay narrowed her eyes as she peered at the Carters' house through the trees.

'Then how the bloody hell did he get away?'

THREE

'KAY – isn't that the bloke who's been on nightshift?'

Glancing up from her mobile phone, trying not to slide across the icy footpath in front of the region's media, Kay looked to where Higgins pointed to see an overweight middle-aged man easing himself out from a green four-door car parked on the driveway next door to the Carters' house.

'Let's have a word before we head back to Sharp,' she said, already marching ahead. 'Excuse me?'

The man paused, an overflowing shopping bag in one hand and a large takeout coffee cup in the other. He seemed bewildered by all the police activity in the crescent and frowned as she drew near.

'What's going on?'

Kay introduced herself and Higgins. 'And you are?'

'Ryan West. What's going on?'

'Shall we talk inside? Away from all the cameras?'

She didn't wait for a response and guided him to the front door of number two, Higgins following.

West's home held an air of neglect, as if the house was missing something – or someone.

Dust covered the top of the radiator in the hallway and clung to the paintwork between the stair balustrades, and Kay wrinkled her nose at a large patch of damp on the ceiling outside the kitchen.

'Do you live here alone, Mr West?' said Higgins as he shut the door.

The man leaned against the doorframe leading to the kitchen and shrugged. 'My wife and I split six months ago. We're trying to sell the place.'

'Mr West, we're investigating the suspicious death of your neighbour, Liz Carter, earlier this morning—'

Kay's words were cut short by West's sharp intake of breath.

'Liz? When?'

'That's what we're trying to establish, Mr

West. Can you confirm where you were this morning?'

'At work.' He straightened as Higgins opened his notebook. 'You can ask them. It's the food distribution place over at Park Wood.'

'Thank you, Mr West. What time did your shift start?'

'Eight o'clock last night. I got there at half seven though, same as I always do. I like to check in with the previous shift before they leave, in case there are any problems.'

'And what do you do there?'

'I'm a forklift driver.'

'And what time did you get home?'

His eyes narrowed. 'You saw me get here.'

'Did you come home at any time before that?'

'No – why would I?'

'Any problems with your neighbours?'

'Liz and Andrew? No – never. We get on all right. They were a bit shocked when the wife left, but Andrew's good at mowing the front lawn for me if he's doing his, and I help him out with bits and pieces from time to time.'

Kay kept her gaze steady. 'And what about your neighbours at the bottom of your garden? The house in the street behind?'

He threw up his hands. 'You've been talking to the Starlings, haven't you? S'pose they told you about the parties last summer?'

'It might've been mentioned.'

'I didn't mean any harm by it. I just had a few mates around when the wife left. They wanted to try and cheer me up. We only had a few drinks. I suppose the music did get a bit loud at one point.'

'Just drinks?'

West flushed. 'Okay, one of my mates might've had a joint. I may have had a puff or two.'

'What about the other neighbours here in the crescent?'

He exhaled and dropped his hands to his sides, evidently relieved that the questioning had moved on. 'Next door at number one is fine – that's Carol. Deaf as a post, but easy to get on with. Jeff and Nicole Bernsen live over at number four. I think there might have been an altercation between Jeff and Andrew a few months ago but to be honest that's been brewing for a while – they're always arguing about the parking along here, especially now that both the Bernsens' kids have their own cars, too.'

'And number five, on the end?'

'Don't know – haven't seen either of them

for a few days. Might be away or something, I suppose.'

Kay watched him for a moment, then pulled out a business card and handed it to him. 'Thanks for your time, Mr West. We'll be in touch if we have further questions. If you do think of something that might help with our enquiries, please call me at this number.'

She led the way back down the driveway, ignoring the shouted questions from the throng of journalists as Sharp and Christie emerged from the Bernsens' house, their faces grim.

'How did you two get on?' said Sharp, leading them under the crime scene tape at the end of the Carters' driveway and pausing beside the garage door.

'Apart from a complaint about loud music and recreational use of cannabis, not much to report.' Kay updated him with what the Starlings and Ryan West had told them, then jerked her chin at the house next door. 'West mentioned the Carters and the Bernsens didn't see eye to eye about the parking here. He said there was some sort of argument about it a few months ago?'

'Jeff Bernsen already told us,' said Christie. 'His kids – Shaun and Jessica – both got their own cars in the summer, and it turned into a car park out here. Sounds like things got heated when one of the kids blocked the Carters' driveway and Andrew couldn't get out to go to work.'

'We'll check Andrew's side of the story before we leave here,' said Sharp, 'just in case there's more to it than Bernsen's version.'

Kay frowned. 'It's a long way from a parking dispute to murder though, isn't it, Sarge?'

'So is playing loud music and smoking the occasional joint.'

FOUR

KAY TUGGED her sweater sleeves over her wrists and blew on her hands as she turned away from a darkening winter sky beyond the incident room windows.

The radiator under the sill choked out warmth but did little to stem the draught from the door opening and closing with each arriving officer, and the hum of fan heaters under desks fought with the clacking of fingers on keyboards and phones ringing.

The air was thick with the smell of damp clothes drying out, and a line of woollen gloves covered the top of the radiator beside the photocopier on the opposite wall.

The team had returned from the Carters' home an hour ago leaving behind the FLO and a pair of uniformed constables to keep a stubborn media at bay.

Kay and her colleagues had spent the time since at their computers adding all the gathered statements and reports into the HOLMES2 database and following up various threads of information that would create the basis of their investigation.

She rubbed at her eyes and bit back a yawn as Higgins wandered over, two steaming mugs of tea in his hand.

'Thanks, Simon. Do you want to sit near the front?'

'Sounds good.'

DS Sharp paced the thin carpet tiles in front of the whiteboard as the team shuffled into their seats, mumbled conversations falling silent as he turned to face them, his expression determined.

'I have to report to DI Larch within the hour,' he began, 'so let's make this a productive session. With regard to the remaining neighbours in the crescent, what else have we learned since this morning?'

Higgins raised his hand. 'Sarge, I got in touch with the resident at the first house – Carol Abbott. When I went round there, another woman opened the door who introduced herself as her daughter, Grace. Mrs Abbott is partially deaf and says she spends a lot of her time sitting in an armchair next to the living room window that faces the street. She confirmed that she didn't see anyone leaving the Carters' house this morning between quarter to eight and eight-fifteen.'

Sharp's brow creased. 'Is she absolutely certain about the timing?'

'Yes, she said she was having a cup of coffee while she was waiting for Grace to arrive to help her with her shopping this morning. They confirmed it's a weekly fixture for them. They left before the first responders arrived and had no idea what happened until they got back home.'

'We've also confirmed that the neighbours at number five, the last house in the crescent, are away at the moment,' said DC Christie. 'They left for Salzburg two days ago to visit the Christmas markets, and won't be back until the weekend.'

Sharp's shoulders slumped as he turned and drew a cross through the outline of their house on the whiteboard and then repeated the action for Carol Abbott's home before tapping the pen on the outline of house number four. 'What did Andrew Carter have to say about the altercation with Jeff Bernsen and the parking?'

'He was embarrassed,' said Christie, 'and said it was something that got blown out of proportion at the time. He said he apologised to Jeff a couple of days later, and everything has been all right since. They were even talking about getting together for drinks on Christmas Eve.'

'Remind me what Andrew Carter does for a living.'

'He's an architect, Sarge.' Christie cleared his throat as he flicked through his notes. 'He's a partner in a small practice based in Sevenoaks – he and another bloke, Alan Cross, set it up six years ago and have a graduate student working for them part-time as well as a full-time admin assistant.'

'Any problems there?'

'None as far as any of them are aware when I spoke to them this afternoon,' Christie said, and turned the page. 'Liz worked as a legal secretary for a firm in Maidstone who specialise in environmental law. Again, no problems to report – and Andrew said that neither of them had received any threats.'

Sharp shoved his hands in his pockets, raised his gaze to the ceiling and exhaled before eyeing his team once more. 'All right, then – the obvious question. Did Andrew Carter kill his wife?'

Christie gestured to the whiteboard. 'Michael and Stephanie Carter confirm that their mother called out from the kitchen at eight o'clock and told them to get a move on – Stephanie said she remembers checking the time on her mobile phone. The kids also confirmed that their dad didn't come into the living room until ten past eight to use his mobile to call 999, so he's the only suspect we've got at the moment. Otherwise, how did someone get into the Carters' house, kill Liz, and leave without being seen? It's impossible.'

'There was no weapon near her body or in the house,' said Kay, 'and the CSIs have confirmed they finished their search of the garage and garden shed half an hour ago. If Andrew killed his wife, what did he do with the weapon? Both kids' statements confirm he stayed with them as soon as he found Liz until the ambulance arrived, so he didn't have time to hide it anywhere else.'

A hush descended on the room as her words sank in.

'We wait for the post mortem results,' said Sharp. 'Maybe Lucas Anderson will find something.'

'Do you think Carter poisoned her, Sarge?' Higgins leaned forward and jerked his chin at the list of names on the board. 'Perhaps she simply hit her head when she passed out.'

'It's a good point,' said the detective

sergeant, 'except that when Lucas was at the scene before you got there he reckoned the damage to her head was caused by a heavy blow rather than the fall.'

Kay chewed the end of her pen as Sharp called the briefing to a close, then wandered back to her desk as an idea began to form.

'Kay?'

She held up her hand to stop Christie interrupting and waved him to a seat beside her as she logged in to the database and typed in Ryan West's name.

Seconds later, she grinned in triumph and spun the screen around to face the older DC.

'I knew his name rang a bell,' she said. 'West was given a restraining order six months ago.'

Christie frowned as he read the text accompanying the man's photograph. 'It says here that his ex-wife filed it.'

'When uniform arrived at the scene, I don't suppose anyone noticed whether there were tread marks in the snow on his driveway?'

He frowned and pushed back his chair. 'I'll have to check. Hang on.'

Kay watched as he hurried over to a pair of constables who were headed out of the door, spoke to the male officer and then gestured for him to join them.

'Kay, this is Rob Paige – he and Lisa Nash were first on scene this morning.'

'Rob, did you notice whether there were any fresh tyre tracks in the driveway next door when you got there?'

Paige pulled out his mobile phone and scrolled through the photos. 'Here. I went outside and took a panoramic shot of the crescent while Lisa was talking to the family.'

Kay took the phone from him and exhaled before holding it up to show Christie, her heart pounding.

'There are tread marks on West's driveway. That doesn't make sense,' she said. 'It started snowing at eight o'clock last night, right?'

'Right. Where are you going with this?'

'If it didn't start snowing until he was already at work, then there shouldn't have been any tyre prints in his driveway until he got home when we saw him – they would've been covered up, wouldn't they?'

Christie's eyes narrowed. 'I think we need to have another chat with Mr West.'

FIVE

KAY OPENED the car door before Christie had applied the handbrake, her jaw set as she stalked around the front of the car and waited for him to climb out.

Fine snowflakes stuck to her hair and clung to her wool coat, obscuring the arc lights that shone over the warehouse car park and six articulated trucks parked outside loading bays.

A peacefulness enveloped the industrial park, the snow muting the sounds emanating from the low-slung brick building that housed the food distribution company.

'I'll lead this one,' Christie said, aiming the key fob over his shoulder as they hurried towards a set of open roller doors. 'Give me a signal if you notice something I don't, or if you want to jump in with a question. We'll keep this formal, but I don't want to make him nervous. According to Sharp, Andrew Carter is still a suspect, too.'

'Will do. Are you going to the post mortem in the morning?'

'Yes. Want to come?'

She grimaced. 'Only if you need me.'

'I'll let you continue going through the statements. We'll catch up when I get back if you like?'

'Sounds good, thanks.'

'Here we go.' He held up his warrant card to a man in an orange high visibility vest who emerged from a small office to the left of the doors and walked towards them. 'We're looking for Ryan West.'

'Can't he talk to you later? He's working.'

'And we're investigating a murder so it won't wait.' Christie cocked his head to one side. 'I'm sure you understand.'

The man swallowed, then pointed to where a forklift was moving back and forth between floor-to-ceiling shelves stacked with crates of tomatoes and lettuces. 'He's over there. You'll need to complete a health and safety assessment first, though – I can't have you wandering around here without it.'

'Tell you what,' said Christie, nodding towards the open office door. 'Why don't we wait in there, and you tell Ryan to join us? It'll be safer that way, and save us some time as well.'

The man exhaled before turning away.

'What if West makes a run for it?' said Kay, glancing over her shoulder as she followed Christie into the office.

'He won't get far.' Christie leaned against a wall and ran his gaze over the paperwork pinned to a corkboard beside him. 'Anyway, we know where he lives, right?'

Moments later, Ryan West entered the room wiping his hands on a rag and wearing a sullen expression.

'Mr West, take a seat.' Christie spun around the single chair in the office, the castors rattling as if about to fall off, and patted his hand on the back of it. 'Hopefully this won't take a minute.'

'I'll stand, thanks.' West flipped the rag over his shoulder and crossed his arms over his chest. 'What do you want?'

'Very well.' Christie recited the formal caution, his voice level. 'We'd like you to explain where you were last night.'

Kay heard West swallow, then stepped towards the doorway as the man's gaze shifted. 'Just tell us the truth, Ryan.'

He emitted a strangled groan, then shook

his head. 'I knew I should've said something this morning. I knew it'd look worse when you found out.'

She remained silent, taking her cue from Christie as West stared at his feet for a moment.

'I forgot my asthma inhaler,' he said as his gaze lifted to hers. 'I went back home for it, that's all.'

'What time?' said Christie.

'About ten o'clock, I suppose.' West nodded towards the computer. 'Derek'll have the exact time I clocked off on there. You can check with him.'

'When did you get back here?' said Kay.

'Just after eleven.'

Christie frowned. 'It doesn't take that long to get to your house from here and back.'

'I couldn't find it when I got there. Took me a while to remember it was up in the bathroom, not where I usually leave it.'

Christie straightened and pushed the chair away as he moved to the door. 'Next time, Mr West, I'd appreciate it if you told us everything.'

'Sorry.'

As Kay followed the more experienced detective constable back to their car, she clutched her coat around her as a fresh flurry of snow scampered around her heels, and bit back a rising sense of frustration.

'Do you think he was telling the truth?' she said, launching herself at the heating controls as soon as Christie started the engine.

'Yes,' he said, 'but whether he was telling us everything remains to be seen. I still think he's hiding something from us.'

SIX

'Based on what you're telling me, we don't have enough evidence to arrest Ryan West at this time.'

DS Sharp pushed himself away from his perch on a desk close to the whiteboard and peered at the updating notes that Christie added in capital letters.

Kay blew across the top of her coffee and then stifled a yawn.

The incident room was quiet save for their muted conversation, the computer screens blank and only the sound of the custody suite on the ground floor filtering up the stairs to where the three of them gathered to review the case to date.

An occasional siren bleated from the street outside as a patrol vehicle swept out from the car park behind the police station, but otherwise an uneasy peace had descended on the town.

'Not at the moment,' Christie said, a note of frustration seeping into his words, 'but he was nervous about something. We just haven't found out what yet.'

'Okay, keep your eyes and ears open,' said Sharp, turning away from the board. 'And don't be hanging around here for much longer tonight. There's another storm heading this way, and I'd rather you both got home safely.'

Christie flicked his wrist, his eyes widening as he saw the time. He swept his coat off the back of his chair, loosened his tie and jerked his thumb towards the door. 'Speaking of which, I'm a dead man if I don't get going – it's our anniversary.'

'Regards to the missus,' said Sharp over his shoulder, already heading back to his desk.

'See you tomorrow.' Kay watched the detective constable leave, then wandered over to the small kitchenette at the back of the room, rinsed out her coffee mug and left it to drain.

At her desk, she tidied the reports that had been left for her and ran her gaze across the sticky notes stuck to her screen and keyboard that jostled for space with memos requiring her urgent attention.

She wiggled her toes to encourage some circulation back into her extremities and tried to remember if there was anything in the freezer to eat when she got home.

Probably not.

Picking up a manila folder, she flipped it open and found print-outs of all the statements taken by the investigating team that morning as they worked their way around the crescent.

She found the one for house number four and rested her chin in her hand as she read through Jeff Bernsen's statement, followed by those of his adult children – all of whom were shocked by the brutal slaying of Liz Carter, despite any previous disagreements between them.

Kay flipped the page and started to read the final statement, that of Nicole Bernsen.

Then stopped.

Flicked back to the beginning and read it again.

'Sarge?'

She peered over her computer screen to where Sharp sat with his back to the wall, his jaw clenched as he read through his emails, and pushed back her chair, Nicole Bernsen's statement in her hand.

'Sarge – can I run something by you?'

He jumped at the sound of her voice, then recovered. 'I thought you'd left when Christie went.'

'Just going through some last-minute paperwork.' She held out the witness statement. 'Can you take a look at this? When you and Christie spoke to Nicole Bernsen this morning, she said that she was looking out her bedroom window at eight oh four this morning and saw Liz out on her patio holding the cat.'

Sharp took the statement from her and ran his eyes over the typed text. 'That's right. It ties in with the Carters' kids' statement that it had escaped the house and she had gone out after it.'

'How could Nicole Bernsen be so sure about the timing?'

'She said it's her morning routine to wander around while she brushes her teeth, and that she saw the time on the alarm clock beside the bed when she turned away from the window to go back into the en suite. Why?'

Kay sighed. 'It means the timeframe

within which Liz Carter could've been murdered is even smaller than we thought…'

The detective sergeant groaned. 'Because Andrew called 999 at ten past eight.'

'Right – so how did Liz's killer get in and out of the garden in under six minutes without being seen?'

SEVEN

When Kay returned to the incident room the next morning, Sharp was already briefing the team about her findings from the previous night.

A few faces looked her way as she found a seat at the end of the semi-circle of chairs in front of the whiteboard and pulled out her notebook, but soon returned their attention to the detective sergeant.

She huffed her fringe from her eyes, trying to calm her heart rate after running up the stairs two at a time, cursing the traffic accident on the main road between Wateringbury and Maidstone that had created a tailback an hour long.

Save for the scratch of pens on paper, the only sound in the room was that of Sharp's voice and as she heard him recite her findings from Nicole Bernsen's statement, her cheeks flushed.

A guilt seeped into the confidence she'd felt when she left last night, an overwhelming awareness that she hadn't helped her colleagues, and only created another problem – and more work.

'How are we getting on with CCTV cameras near the bus stop on the street beyond the crescent?'

Sharp's question jolted Kay from her thoughts and she looked across as a young uniformed constable rose from his chair.

'We've received it this morning, Sarge,' he said, 'so I'll make a start as soon as the briefing's done.'

'Let me know the minute you find anything, and—' Sharp broke off and turned his attention to the back of the room. 'What is it, Maurice?'

Kay turned to see Sergeant Hoyle hovering at the door, a sheaf of paperwork in his hand.

'Thought you might want to know – I was going through the call logs from Monday night and checking them off against the system. One of our community officers was called out to Ryan West's wife's home at quarter past ten – says here he breached a restraining order.'

Kay's eyes locked with Christie's as the detective constable pushed back his chair.

'He told us he left work that night because he forgot his asthma inhaler,' he said.

'Which makes me wonder what else he might be lying about,' said Sharp. 'Best you and Kay get yourselves over there now.'

EIGHT

THE THICK SNOW was starting to retreat by the time Kay parked the pool vehicle next to the kerb outside Ryan West's house.

Her boots sank into a soft slush as she got out and peered over the car roof at the second house in the crescent, a weak sunlight blinking in and out of grey clouds that promised rain before the end of the day.

She shivered and hurried to join Christie as he strode towards the front door and beat his fist against the metal letterbox set into the wooden surface.

'He's probably asleep,' she murmured, gesturing to the drawn curtains across the front windows, both downstairs and at the bedrooms above.

'Hope so,' Christie said, his eyes hard.

She turned back to the door at the sound

of footfalls thudding down the stairs, then a security chain rattled.

A bleary-eyed Ryan West peered out at them, a confused expression turning indignant.

'What do you want now?'

'Can we come in, Mr West?' said Christie, taking a step forward.

West moved, shifting his body to block the detective constable. 'What's this about?'

'You missed out some vital information when we spoke to you at work last night. Specifically, the fact that you lied about your whereabouts between the hours of ten and eleven o'clock.'

Christie cocked an eyebrow, waiting for the man's response.

'All right.' West moved to one side, and slammed the door the moment they both stood in the hallway. 'Come through here.'

Kay followed the two men into a spartan living room, the bookshelves bare and a lighter shade of paint on the wall where once a large television had been.

West stopped in the middle of the room and turned to face them.

'Look, I did come home to get my inhaler. I just stayed a bit longer – to calm down before I went back to work, that's all.' He exhaled and rubbed his hands down his face. 'I know I was stupid, trying to approach Ann-Marie before I came back here – I suppose it's because of the time of year – we used to love Christmas together, and now look at me.'

Kay snapped her notebook closed as Christie let out a sigh.

'Don't leave town without letting us know, Mr West,' he said. 'And keep away from your ex-wife.'

'Do you think he's telling the truth?' said Kay as her colleague closed the front door and led the way across the driveway to their vehicle at the kerb.

'About being an idiot? Yes.' Christie pulled the keys from his pocket and unlocked the car. 'As to whether that makes him capable of murder, I'm not sure.'

'What if—' Kay broke off as the front door to number three opened, and PC Alice Brooks, the Family Liaison Officer peered out and beckoned them over. 'Everything all right?'

'Mr Carter spotted you arriving,' said the FLO, 'and wondered if you could come in? He's quite anxious to speak with you both.'

'Okay.'

She followed Christie into the living room, a retro-fitted multi-fuel burning stove in the corner of the far wall creating a cocoon of warmth offset by a heavy atmosphere of grief that permeated the whole space.

A television played silently in the corner, the sports channel ignored as three faces turned to her and then Andrew Carter rose from his seat and held out his hand.

'Richard, thanks for dropping in.'

'Not at all,' said Christie, and introduced Kay to the family. 'Alice said you wanted a word?'

'Actually, it's Michael here who wanted to speak with you.' Andrew beckoned to his teenage son. 'Come on, they don't bite.'

Kay smiled at the man's gentle tone and turned her attention to the fifteen-year-old who was already the same height as his father, but who hung back with the reluctance of someone not used to being in the spotlight.

Christie's face softened as he nodded to the boy. 'It's true, we don't bite. What did you want to talk to us about, Michael?'

The teenager blushed. 'I only remembered it when Dad mentioned you were outside,' he said, his voice breaking. He cleared his throat, blinked back tears. 'It might be nothing, of course.'

'Let us worry about that,' said Christie. 'Is it something about yesterday?'

Michael nodded, then wiped his eyes with

his sleeve. 'We were in here, watching the telly while we were having breakfast as usual. Dad was up in the shower. Jesse – that's the cat – he's not meant to be outside for another week but he was in the kitchen with Mum. I think she must've forgotten he was there –

she's always rushing around in the mornings…' He broke off, gulped in a breath. 'There was a break in the adverts on TV – just a few seconds before the programme came back on, and that's when I heard it.'

'What did you hear?' said Andrew, placing his hand on his son's arm.

'That's the thing. I'm not sure. It sounded something like one of those hang gliders with a small engine, y'know?'

Kay frowned. 'Do you mean a microlight?'

'Yeah, that's it. Anyway, a moment later Jesse managed to get past Mum and out the back door while she was checking what the weather was doing, and then…'

The teenager turned away, burying his face into his father's chest while his shoulders heaved with sobs.

Kay turned to Christie, the confused expression in his eyes mirroring her own tumbling thoughts.

What was a microlight doing flying in this weather?

NINE

'Come on, I need to get something for lunch and you need to eat, too.'

Kay grinned as Higgins hovered next to her desk, her stomach rumbling as her eyes found the time displayed in the corner of her computer screen.

'Sounds like a plan.'

She locked the screen, plucked her coat off the back of her chair and followed him out of the door, squinting as a cold blast of air assaulted her face when they got outside.

'What d'you fancy?' said Higgins, leading the way across the busy main road and up the pedestrianised cobblestones of Gabriel's Hill. 'Sandwich or pie?'

'Something hot. And full of carbs.'

'You'll be moaning about that in a few months when it starts to warm up.'

'I'm willing to risk it.' She followed him into a café to their right at the top of the hill, the windows wet with condensation and a cosy warmth inside.

Passing the smattering of wooden tables along the wall to her left, Kay made her way to the glass counter next to the till and eyed the display of hot pastries.

She picked out two sausage rolls, ordered coffee and moved to a table near the window while Higgins bought his lunch.

Beyond the glass, the pavements were crowded with office workers seeking out their lunches or running errands within their allotted one-hour break.

Sighing as she took the first bite, Kay eased back into her seat as Higgins joined her, and passed him a ketchup sachet.

'Thanks. What are you doing for Christmas this year?' he said between mouthfuls. 'Any plans?'

She wrinkled her nose. 'I've signed up to work through the holiday.'

'Seriously?'

'I figured it'd be easier than spending it with my parents.' She forced a smile. 'Besides, there's only me at home – it makes sense that I take on the shifts rather than someone with a family and kids.'

'I reckon by Boxing Day, some of those will be wishing they're at work instead.'

Kay laughed, then licked the grease from her fingers before crunching up the paper bag. While she savoured the coffee, her gaze returned to the street as a uniformed patrol passed and she held up her hand in greeting.

When she turned back, Higgins was staring into space, his chicken pie halfway to his mouth.

'Are you all right?' she said.

He blinked, then lowered the pie and leaned forward, lowering his voice.

'I think I know who killed Liz Carter.'

TEN

'It was us talking about Christmas that made me think of it.'

Higgins stood beside Sharp in front of the whiteboard, and tapped the enlarged map showing the crescent where the Carters lived and the neighbouring properties.

Kay sat on the edge of her seat, battening down her excitement as her colleague spoke to the gathered investigative team, his initial nerves disappearing as he warmed to his theory.

'Go on,' said Sharp.

'When Kay and I spoke to Hugh and Beverley Starling, we noticed he's an avid modeller – you know, airplanes and the like. He said he was building a Spitfire at the moment, and that if he finished it before

Christmas, he was hoping their kids would buy him some more kits to work on.'

'What does that have to do with Liz Carter?' said Christie.

'His wife mentioned Hugh builds radio-controlled boats – I took a look at them while Kay was talking to his wife outside.' Higgins paused, then shuffled his feet as his face turned red. 'Anyway, I wanted to check the side gate to see if anyone had gone through there to access the Carters' garden and when he showed me through the garage to get to it, there was one of those radio-controlled drones on a workbench next to their car. It looked damaged. I just wondered if—'

'—Starling was messing about with it that morning, and lost control. Factor in the height it dropped from plus velocity, and Liz wouldn't have known what hit her,' said Sharp, his voice full of wonder.

'And it could be the case that Hugh Starling has no idea he's responsible for her death,' said Kay. 'I mean, it would've only taken seconds. If he did something with the controls, or the cold weather affected the drone's responsiveness, he might've re-established control and flown it back to his garden none the wiser.'

Sharp clapped Higgins on the shoulder. 'Good work, Simon.'

Kay nodded to her colleague as he took a seat beside her, the incident room buzzing with an excited white noise.

'Let's have some quiet and work through this,' said Sharp, his voice rising to be heard. He turned to Kay. 'What about when you were outside in the Starlings' back garden – notice anything?'

'There were a lot of footprints, Sarge, but none near the hedgerow or trees that border the Carters' garden. When I asked whose they were, Hugh Starling said they were his and that he'd been out feeding the birds and taking out food rubbish to the compost bin.' She frowned. 'He never mentioned the drone.'

'Well, according to the guidance that comes with those things, he shouldn't have been flying it out there,' said Christie. 'That's if he's got a licence for it – it's not compulsory at the moment.'

'We're going to have to be careful with this. At the moment, we have a theory but no evidence to support it – yet.' Sharp loosened his tie as his eyes met Kay's. 'Let's bring Hugh Starling in for questioning – and tell him he'll need a solicitor present.'

ELEVEN

Kay showed Hugh Starling and his solicitor into interview room two, closed the door and crossed to the table where Sharp sat, his face impassive.

Starling and his wife were shaken by the police turning up on their doorstep, more so when Hugh was asked to attend Maidstone station for questioning.

Starling fetched the drone from his garage without a fuss, confusion in his voice as he handed it over to Higgins, who then guided him to the waiting patrol car.

Even now, when Kay glanced at the man as she entered the room, she could sense his bewilderment.

The shoebox-sized drone was now enclosed within a see-through evidence bag, which Kay placed on the table while she took her seat beside the detective sergeant and switched on the recording machine.

As Sharp cited the formal caution, she ran her gaze over the sides of the drone's plastic moulding and frowned at the scuff marks on one side, a dark substance smeared beside the right-hand landing gear.

'Mr Starling, we have some questions in relation to the events of Monday morning and the death of Liz Carter,' Sharp began. 'When my colleague DC Hunter spoke with you and asked about the footprints in the snow in your back garden, could you please confirm what you said?'

Starling cleared his throat and leaned forward, his hands in his lap. 'Of course. I went out to top up the bird feeders and empty the food scraps into the compost bin.'

'Did you do anything else out there that morning? Perhaps something you failed to mention to DC Hunter at the time?'

'I-I only didn't mention it because Beverley would've been cross,' he said. 'She's been nagging me not to fly the drone in the garden but the radio transmitter was playing up last time I took it down to the park and I spent the weekend fixing it. I just wanted to give it a quick test flight to see if it worked.'

'And did it?'

Starling nodded. 'For the first couple of minutes, yes. I got it up to about ten feet…' He broke off, frowned. 'But then the signal was lost. I don't know what happened. Bloody nuisance, to be honest.'

'What did you do next?' said Sharp.

The detective sergeant kept his hands flat on the manila folder, but Kay could sense the tension emanating from him.

She held her breath.

'Well, that's the thing. I was trying to get the drone to come back to me and land it but it went up another couple of feet, then shot across the tree line.'

Sharp flipped open the folder and pushed an aerial photograph of the area across the table. 'Could you show me on here the direction it went?'

Starling reached out. 'Here. Across the border with the Carters. Then I lost sight of it – nothing was working with the controls.'

'How long was the drone out of control?'

'Not long. Perhaps a minute. Then – I don't know – something in one of the switches gave under my touch and I could hear it again. It appeared above the trees, and I was able to fly it back. Landed it next to the kitchen door as I heard Beverley turn off the shower upstairs.'

Sharp turned the evidence bag around. 'These markings on the drone here, were they there before or after you flew it on Monday?'

'Afterwards.' Starling sighed. 'It's covered in mud or something as well – I put it out in the garage before Beverley came downstairs. I'll fix it next time she's out shopping with her friends next week. She'll be asking me what I was doing with it otherwise.'

'What time was this?'

Starling shifted in his seat. 'Just after eight o'clock, I suppose. Beverley's morning routine is like clockwork so she would've been in the bathroom at eight.'

'And so that's when you decided to sneak out and test the drone while she wasn't looking?'

'Yes.'

'Mr Starling…' Sharp paused, glancing at the man's solicitor for a moment, then back to the pensioner. 'There's no easy way to tell you this, but we have reason to believe that your drone was responsible for the death of Liz Carter on Monday morning.'

Starling paled, his eyes wide. 'That – that can't be true.'

Sharp patted the evidence bag. 'We're going to run some tests on this but believe me, I've seen enough blood in my time doing this job to recognise it when I see it, and this isn't mud. Liz Carter was killed by someone – or something – that managed to enter her garden within a six-minute timeframe and leave no footprints in thick snow. One of her children reported hearing a buzzing noise at the time, something with a small motor – such as a drone.' Sharp closed the manila folder, a sadness in his voice as he continued. 'Based on our conversation and the evidence to hand, I have to conclude that you were responsible for her death.'

Kay heard Starling's sharp intake of breath as he raised a shaking hand to his mouth.

'I didn't know I killed anyone. I didn't know I killed Liz.'

'Nevertheless, Mr Starling I am obliged to read you your rights and explain what will happen next.'

Hugh Starling held his hands to his grief-stricken face, sobs wracking his shoulders as Sharp's words rang out in the small room.

TWELVE

Kay filed the last of her reports to the database folder for the investigation, the satisfaction of a murder case being successfully closed tinged with a bittersweet sense of loss.

A subdued atmosphere hung in the air after Sharp explained to the investigating team that they had found their killer, a silence descending while administrative staff and uniformed officers tidied their desks, a palpable shock underlying their mumbled conversations.

It had fallen to Christie to call Beverley Starling and advise that her husband was under arrest for suspicion of killing Liz Carter, the woman's wails audible as he'd held his phone away from his ear before calming her as best he could.

Sharp had spoken to Andrew Carter, his face ashen when he returned from the family home.

'Some Christmas they're going to have,' said Higgins, his voice little more than a murmur as he packed paperwork and folders into boxes ready to be passed on to the Crown Prosecution Service in the New Year.

'Two families…' Kay shook her head. 'All because of an accident.'

'So he really had no idea?'

'None at all – Hoyle has put a suicide watch on his cell tonight, just in case.'

Higgins placed the boxes on the floor beside her desk and leaned on the topmost one. 'Are you going to be all right? You've been quiet ever since you and Sharp came back upstairs after the interview.'

'I will be.' She forced a smile, switched off her computer and pulled on her wool coat, flicking her hair over the collar. 'Safe drive home, Simon.'

'You too.'

Outside in the car park, Kay raised her gaze to the fresh flurry of snowflakes drifting in front of the streetlights beyond the security barrier, tiny prickles of ice catching on her eyelids as she inhaled the crisp air.

Her phone rang, shattering the peace.

Fishing it out from her bag, she smiled when she recognised her neighbour's name on the display.

'Jas? Everything all right?' Music played in the background, something with a piano, and she could hear the clink of glassware somewhere close by over muted conversations. 'Where are you?'

'I'm in Maidstone – Peter fancied a drink somewhere and a change of scenery. We found this lovely little bar off East Street. We thought you might like to join us, if you've finished for the day?'

'I don't know, Jasmina,' she said, a sense of panic rising in her chest as she headed towards her car. 'I wouldn't want to encroach on your date night. Besides, it's been a busy week and we've got a long day ahead of us tomorrow…'

'When was the last time you went out?' Jasmina demanded. 'I mean, out properly, not just our usual catch-up?'

'Well…'

'Exactly. Come on. Get yourself over here. Just have one, if you must. It's nearly Christmas, after all. Besides…' she lowered her voice, and Kay could hear her making her excuses as she found somewhere quieter to talk. 'There's someone I want you to meet. A friend of Peter's. I think you'll like him.'

'Jas, if you're trying to…'

'He's a vet, Kay.'

'A vet?' Kay opened the car door and slipped behind the wheel.

'You know, animals and stuff.'

'I know what a vet does, Jas.'

'He's good looking, too.'

Despite herself, despite the tiredness that crawled through her system, Kay smiled at her friend's attempts to cajole her into being more sociable and turned the key in the ignition.

'Well, in that case…'

THE END

ABOUT THE AUTHOR

Rachel Amphlett is a USA Today bestselling author of crime fiction and spy thrillers, many of which have been translated worldwide.

Her novels are available in eBook, print, and audiobook formats from libraries and retailers as well as her website shop.

A keen traveller, Rachel has both Australian and British citizenship.

Find out more about Rachel's books at: www.rachelamphlett.com.

Ingram Content Group UK Ltd.
Milton Keynes UK
UKHW011300120323
418437UK00004B/390